Andy's Discovery

Andy's Discovery
Matthew C. Benjamin
Copyright 2003. All rights reserved

First Paperback Edition, August 2003

Illustrations and cover design by Mia del Conte
Tractor photographs courtesy of Deere & Company

Published by
Adventure & Discovery Press
Franklin Square Station
P.O. Box 11746
Syracuse, NY 13218

Printed in the United States of America by Quartier Printing, New York

Library of Congress Cataloguing-in-Publication Data

CIP applied for

ISBN 0-9744672-0-0

Andy's Discovery

by Matthew C. Benjamin
illustrated by Mia del Conte

American Boy Collection
Cooperstown, New York

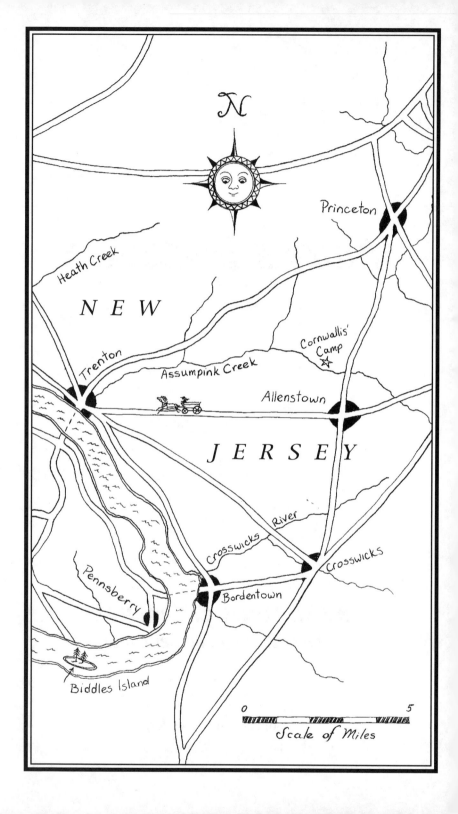

To all individuals who protect us and our freedom.
American Heroes.

Table of Contents

Grandpa Jack Reveals

Andy's grandpa Jack Mott was born on the family farm and worked the land for over 50 years. Andy recently turned twelve years old and was curious about everything. The farm has been in their family for 10 generations and is located south of the city of Trenton, in the state of New Jersey.

Often, during quiet summer days, Andy and his grandpa would sit on the porch together. They would recall how everything had changed on the farm. The new machinery and fertilizers have made farming especially more productive, Grandpa would say. Tractors, harvesters, balers, and combines all made work easier. Grandpa Jack would recall his own father working the fields with horses and plows. He also remembered the first tractor and harvester his father purchased in 1938.

But of course, that was many years ago. The farm of Andy's grandpa's childhood was filled with hard work. Now Grandpa Jack and Grandma Helen lived in a retirement community in Trenton. It was a nice place with plenty to do. Instead of plowing and harvesting fields, Grandpa now spent his time playing card games and checkers, reading, and listening to his radio. Grandma still cooked every night and they would go dancing on Friday and Saturday nights. It was satisfying to know that the retirement community had plenty of social activities for its members.

Grandpa and Grandma were blessed with six children and more grandchildren than grandpa had fingers and toes.

Andy was Grandpa Jack's favorite grandson, and was like himself: dreamy, curious and quiet. They would sit for hours on the porch. Grandpa Jack would answer Andy's questions about the world, questions like, "Why are an Asian person's eyes shaped differently than mine? Why are the seasons different in South America? How come a seed which is dead comes alive when planted?"

After lunch one day, Grandpa Jack called his grandson to come sit with him on the porch swing. At this time, Andy's two older brothers, Rick and Dan, were working the fields with their father. Andy had already finished feeding the cows and cleaning the barn earlier that morning. Andy's mother, grandma, and younger sister Missy were all working in the vegetable garden. Andy's mother selected ripe vegetables for dinner. His grandma weeded around the plants and Missy picked fresh strawberries for dessert.

Andy and his grandpa rested on the porch swing in silence until his grandpa sighed.

2

"Andy you know everyone's not chosen to live on a farm," his grandpa began.

"I know that, Grandpa." Andy answered.

"Your grandma and I worked this farm and raised our six children after my father passed it down to me," his grandpa said.

"I know that, Grandpa." Andy said again, in a low tone.

"Your father was blessed with the ability and desire to continue farming our land. And I hope you or your brothers will continue to farm the land," his grandpa continued, with a smile on his face.

"Grandpa, you know that I am interested in carrying on the tradition," Andy replied, as he smiled back at his grandpa.

Then his Grandpa Jack began questioning Andy. "How much do you think this farm is worth?"

"Grandpa, you asked me that question last week," Andy recalled, as he rocked the porch swing a little harder.

"Yes, but that was last week. Last week I had thirty dollars in my wallet and now I have only fifteen. Things change. Some things increase in value. Some things decrease in value. And very seldom does anything stay the same," his grandpa said, waving his hand and shrugging his shoulders.

"So, how much do you think this farm is worth?" Grandpa Jack asked again.

Andy stared out at the farm land a long time

before making a wild guess. "I don't know. A million dollars?" he offered.

"Do you really think so, my boy?" His grandpa said, looking out over the farm.

"What do you think determines the value of this farm?" his grandpa questioned Andy again.

"I guess the house, barns and land," Andy answered. "Also the farm equipment and livestock increase the value of the farm."

Andy thought for a moment, *Father just purchased a new John Deere tractor. He recalled his father explaining to his brothers, "The Model 6420 will increase the farm's efficiency as well as provide the operator with heat or air conditioning during a long day's work in the fields."*

Andy also remembered his brother Rick saying, "We'll still be able to use our Model 4620 for basic chores around the farm." He recalled his brother Dan adding, "We can also add the corn picker to the tractor and harvest some of the smaller fields."

"The new tractor would surely increase the value of the farm!" Andy shouted out.

"The farm is worth more than just a dollar amount," his Grandpa Jack said. "The farm has a value that can't be measured in dollars."

Grandpa Jack continued, "The Mott family has farmed this land since 1750. This farm represents 10 generations of Motts. This farm represents a lifestyle that's been passed down from one generation to the next. This farm represents freedom, too.

The freedom that allows the farmer to take care of the land. The freedom to produce crops and livestock to feed our great country."

Andy listened carefully to every word his Grandpa Jack said, giving his full attention to every detail. Andy knew that America was founded on *Life, Liberty, and the Pursuit of Happiness.* What he didn't know was that his Grandpa Jack had a story to tell. A story that included the family farm, life, and liberty; together with the pursuit of happiness.

"Andy, I want to tell you the history of our farm, the history of your birth name, and how our family fought for *life and liberty,*" his grandpa said.

And the story unfolded like this....

The Secret Letter

The dirt road that ran from Trenton to Allenstown was packed deep with snow, and still more snow was falling. In the summer this 12 mile trip from Trenton to Allenstown by wagon was far. But it was winter now, and the trip seemed even longer and harder.

Andrew Mott couldn't help worrying as the two old farm horses slowly pulled the wagon. Andrew was twelve years old and had many responsibilities on the farm. John Mott, Andrew's father, had been fighting in the war for almost two years - ever since it started, in 1775. He was in General Washington's Continental Army. It seemed to Andrew like the war with England would never end. He looked into the forest on both sides of the road, watching for the British. Andrew felt cold all over, and not just because it was winter. He had made the trip a hundred times before. But this trip was different from all the rest.

Andrew called "Giddyap!" to his team of horses. When he arrived home his father was sitting at the table. He looked deep in thought.

"Andrew," his father said, looking troubled, "A secret letter must be taken to Allenstown. General Washington needs someone who knows the road. Someone the British would never think to question ..." It seemed to Andrew like hours passed before his father spoke again. "Will you do it, Andrew? If you will, General Washington wants to see you tomorrow," Andrew's father said, in a calm voice.

"Tomorrow?" Andrew answered, almost not able to believe what was happening. Sometimes it seemed like nothing ever changed on the farm. But now this! This would change everything! And it was so sudden.

His father sat down and began to clean his gun. Then he spoke once more in a low voice. "Andrew....you know what could happen if the British catch you?"

Andrew thought for a minute. *I would be carrying a secret letter to General Washington.* Andrew's face turned white and his heart missed a beat. *I would be a spy!*

Placing his hand on Andrew's arm, his father spoke softly. "If the British catch you with the letter, they could hang you. If you don't want to do it, General Washington will understand." Andrew's father waited for an answer.

But Andrew Mott said nothing. He was thinking about poor Peter Phillips from Yardville. He was a young *patriot* with a wife and new baby when the British hanged him as a spy last month.

John Mott put down his gun, "I didn't want to ask you," he said, "but there is no one else we can count on, and that letter must get to Allenstown."

Andrew's father walked over to the fire and threw on another log. "Think on it some tonight," he suggested. "I've got to go back to General Washington's camp in the morning. I must know by then." Still Andrew did not answer. He was thinking. Finally his eyes evenly met those of his father.

"I'll do it," he said quietly.

Andrew didn't sleep much that night. *He thought about the war. And about his father. And about Peter Phillips, the young patriot who lost his life. Then he began to think about all the men and women who were fighting and risking their lives for their country. And he thought about liberty. Liberty! That one word seemed to ring in Andrew's mind. He wasn't sure of just what it meant. But he knew it had to do with people being free to think and act as they pleased. He knew it was so important that men and women were willing to die for it! And now he might also die for it.* It was hours before he was finally able to get to sleep.

In the morning Andrew and his father got up before the sun. Andrew's mother, Rose, was already fixing breakfast in the kitchen.

"What about the chickens, Pa?" Andrew asked.

His father smiled. "Your mother can feed the chickens today. You and I have important work to do." He put his arm around Andrew.

9

Andrew and his father ate breakfast without talking much. Then they got the horses ready and rode out together to General Washington's camp. The snow was just starting to come down. In the early morning light it was hard to see much of anything.

Suddenly, something jumped right out in front of their horses! It was just a small animal, but it frightened the horses. Andrew's father's horse jumped high in the air. His gun went flying from his hands. It hit the ground and went off with a loud bang. He cried out and fell from his horse.

"Pa!" Andrew cried out. He jumped down from his horse and ran over to where his father lay in the snow. A dark red circle covered the snow under his leg. Andrew took one look at the blood and ran back to his horse. Taking a piece of rope from his saddle, he returned to his father.

"Just above the wound," his father said. "Tie the rope just above where you see the blood." But Andrew was already fast at work. When he finished tying up the wound he helped his father back up on his horse. Andrew could see that he was weak from the gunshot.

"We better get you home, Pa," he urged.

But Andrew's father shook his head.

"I'll be all right, Andrew. It's not far back to the farm. Your mother will know what to do. But you have a meeting with General Washington!"

Andrew's face began to turn red. "By myself,

Pa? I've got to go and meet General Washington by myself?"

"He's a good man, Andrew. A man you can trust same as you would your Pa. Now you get started for the camp. Tell General Washington what happened this morning. Tell him I'll be back as soon as I can," his father said, grinning.

Andrew turned his horse back on the road. He waved to his father, then started out again for General Washington's camp.

He called out, "Giddyap!"

The Road to Allenstown

Andrew kept his horse Ginger at a fast walk. Snow was falling and the air was very cold. His hair was pushed up under his hat. His coat was pulled around his face to protect it against the wind. He had a scarf tied around his head, and his eyes were the only things visible. Right now even his best friend wouldn't have known him. The sun had come up, but with the snow falling, it was still hard to see.

Suddenly, as he rode around a bend in the road, a man jumped out. He was wearing a torn old blue coat. And he was holding a gun.

"Stop!" he shouted.

"Giddyap!" Andrew shouted into Ginger's ear. "Come on, girl, giddyap!" He could see the gun in the man's hands. It was pointed right at his head. He rode right past the man, ducking down low in the saddle. Behind him there was a sharp crack. The shot buzzed by his head like an angry bee. Up the road two more men jumped out of the forest. Their guns were pointed right at him. There was nothing he could do. He would have to let them rob

13

him. Andrew stopped his horse in the road. Slowly he brought his hands up over his head.

"Get down from that horse," a voice barked from behind. It was the first man, the one who had shot at him. "Now take off your scarf so we can see your face." Andrew did as the man ordered.

"Well, I'll be," the man exclaimed when he saw Andrew. By now the other two men had come from up the road. "Hey, Ben! Aaron! Look here," he motioned to them. "It's just a young boy."

Andrew felt himself shake when he saw the hole in his hat. The gunshot had come very close.

"Who are you?" One of the men said to Andrew. "And what business brings you out this way?"

Andrew didn't answer. *Should he tell them? What if they were British?*

Then the first man spoke again. "If he won't talk to us..." He looked at his two friends while he spoke. "...then he is going to have to do his explaining to General Washington."

Andrew looked up in surprise. "General Washington?" he said. "That's who I'm on my way to see." He could feel his heart beating again. "Would you take me to see the General, please? I'm Andrew Mott. He knows I'm coming."

The first man shook his head with a laugh. "Well, I'll be! It's John's son! Boys, you stay here and watch the road. I'll take him to the General."

Before he knew it, Andrew was standing in General Washington's office. It was in a small farm house. General Washington was tall. His eyes were deep and blue.

At first Andrew didn't know what to say. But General Washington did most of the talking. He said he was sorry to hear about Andrew's father. He was also sorry about Andrew's close call. After a short time, Andrew knew that his father had been right about the General. He knew he could trust him.

"Your father explained to you about the letter? It must be taken to Allenstown," General Washington said.

"Yes," Andrew answered. "I understand."

"And you know what could happen to you if you're caught?" General Washington said.

"Yes," Andrew answered again.

"It's not just the British you will have to watch out for," General Washington warned. "There are many people living in Allenstown who side with the British. People who would do anything in their power to stop us from winning the war. They would be happy to turn you over to the British."

Andrew said nothing. General Washington could see that Andrew had made up his mind and would not change it.

The General came over and stood in front of Andrew. "Your father told me that you often make trips to Allenstown for supplies." he said.

"That's right," Andrew said. "People see me on the road all the time."

"That's why I'm sending you with the letter. No one will think that it's strange if you go to pick up supplies. But don't talk to too many people. And be careful of what you say," the General insisted.

General Washington went over to his desk and picked up a small white letter. Handing it to Andrew, he spoke slowly, almost in a whisper. "Take this letter to Emma Minton. She is the seamstress in Allenstown. Wait while she gives you an answer to bring me," he said.

After Andrew had taken the letter, General Washington added, "You're a true *patriot*. The fight for *liberty* is in your hands. Good luck, and God be with you!"

The ride home didn't seem so long. It had stopped snowing, and Andrew was happy. *"The fight for liberty is in your hands,"* the General had said.

He looked up at the cold gray sky. He could tell that there was considerably more snow yet to come. It would make the trip to Allenstown tomorrow long and hard.

When Andrew got back to the farm, his father was resting. His mother had cleaned and taken care of his wound. He was going to be all right. They wanted to know everything that General Washington had said to him. Both his mother and his father were afraid that the British would catch him. Andrew could see it in their eyes. But he could see something else in their eyes, too. Andrew could

see they were pleased he had decided to take part in the fight for *liberty*.

Now Andrew was on his way to Allenstown. "Only a few more hours," he consoled himself. His team of horses pulled the wagon along the road which ran parallel to the Assumpink River. He looked around for British soldiers again. The secret letter was in a special pocket, which his mother had sewn into his coat. Even if he were stopped by the British, they would never find the letter. Or so Andrew hoped.

The British army was camped directly on the Assumpink River, not far from Allenstown. General Cornwallis was the head of the British Army. General Cornwallis was trying to get his army back into fighting shape. They had just lost the Battle of Trenton against General Washington's army.

They lost in part because of the work of American spies. General Cornwallis wasn't planning on losing any more battles. Or letting any more spies get to General Washington.

All this Andrew knew. *He thought about Peter Phillips. He had been caught spying by the British. And they had hanged him.* Andrew became afraid. His blood ran cold. *He thought he heard sounds of horses from far off.* He stopped the wagon and listened intensely.

But it was only the wind and the blowing snow. Andrew kept on looking for British soldiers, but he saw no one.

It was afternoon when he reached Allenstown. His first stop would be Calhoun's Store, where he would buy farm supplies. That was why he had come to Allenstown, at least that was the story he would use to cover up the real reason.

Andrew hoped Mr. Calhoun wouldn't be in the store today. He was a strange man. He had been a friend of his father's before the war. But the two men didn't see things the same way any more. That was all right with Andrew. He never liked Mr. Calhoun anyway. He hoped that his daughter Cara would be in the store instead. Cara was not very pretty, but she was kind of nice in her own way.

Andrew brought the wagon to a stop in front of Calhoun's Store. He tied the horses to the post in front. Stamping the snow from his boots, he went inside. It felt good and warm after his trip. At first the store seemed empty. Andrew looked around the place. He felt cold all over again when Mr. Calhoun came walking slowly out from the back room.

The Seamstress Spy

"Well, now if it isn't Andrew Mott," Alexander Calhoun observed. "What brings you all the way to Allenstown on a day like this? The roads must be pretty bad with all this snow."

Right off Andrew felt like he was in trouble. It was the way Mr. Calhoun made his voice sound.

"We need some supplies for the farm, Mr. Calhoun," Andrew answered quickly back. "Pa thought the snow would hold. I left before it started."

Alexander Calhoun looked closely at Andrew. "How is your Pa?" He asked, almost in a threatening way. "It's been almost a year since I saw him last. Funny he never comes to town anymore."

Andrew knew he had to think fast. "Well, he was sick for a long time. And the axle on the wagon broke. And the roof needed fixing." He wanted to say just enough to Mr. Calhoun. But not too much.

"The axle on the wagon broke?" Mr. Calhoun asked. He seemed interested.

"Yes," Andrew said, looking straight ahead. "It was a big job for Pa, what with being sick and all."

"I guess it would be," Mr. Calhoun agreed. "Tell me, anything much happening down Trenton way? Your Pa have any idea what George Washington is up to? He sure is a funny one, old George." Rubbing his chin, Mr. Calhoun gave a mean laugh. "Those farmers that George calls his army sure are a sad lot."

Andrew could feel his face getting red. But he couldn't let him know how he really felt. "Can't say as how I know much about that, Mr. Calhoun. Things have been pretty busy on the farm. We haven't had much time to keep up with the war." Andrew felt he had himself under control now. "I just hope they all stay clear of our farm. Long as they leave us alone!" Andrew knew that was the kind of talk Mr. Calhoun wanted to hear.

Alexander Calhoun gave a short laugh. "You just wait till General Cornwallis gets hold of those farmers. His army is a *real* army, not a bunch of farmers. Next time the British army will cut those farmers to pieces."

Astonished, Andrew wanted to ask Alexander Calhoun if he had forgotten about the Battle of Trenton, which Washington's army had just won. But he wisely knew it was best to say nothing.

Andrew waited a few seconds and then said, "Now about the supplies..."

Mr. Calhoun got out all the supplies that Andrew needed. Then he helped him put them into the wagon outside.

21

"It's a long trip back to your farm. Why don't you have a cup of tea before you go? I'll just heat up some water," Mr. Calhoun said, reappearing at the door.

"Oh, no thank you," Andrew said right away. "That's very kind of you. But I want to stop off and say hello to my friend Nathan Chapman. Then I better be getting home."

"All right, Andrew," Alexander Calhoun said with a cold smile. "You do that. You go and have a nice visit with your friend Nathan Chapman. Guess you don't get to see much of each other. And have a safe trip home."

Andrew left the wagon in front of the store. It wasn't far to Emma Minton's clothing shop. But he didn't walk right to the shop. Instead he walked toward Nathan Chapman's house. Then he leisurely made his way around to the back of the clothing shop. This way Mr. Calhoun wouldn't see where he was going.

When he got to the shop, Andrew paused outside. The window was filled with beautiful dresses and coats. Emma Minton, the seamstress, had made the dresses and coats with her own hands. Andrew cautiously looked around to make sure no one was watching him. Then he went inside. A young woman sat at a table, working. Andrew looked around the shop until the woman got up from her work. She was tall and slender. Her eyes were deep brown, like her long hair. Andrew's eyes focused

22

on a beautiful gold heart-shaped locket around her neck.

"Good afternoon," she said, coming over to Andrew. "What can I do for you?"

"Miss Minton?" Andrew asked slowly.

"Yes," the seamstress said with a warm smile. "May I help you?"

Andrew looked around again to make sure they were alone in the shop. Then he looked at the seamstress and said in a low voice, *"On land or on sea we shall fight to be free."*

The secret words took Emma Minton by surprise. She rapidly stepped back for a minute. Could this boy really be a spy? She wondered.

There was a look in Andrew's eyes that gave her the answer.

"What be the cause?" she asked. This was the second part of the secret greeting.

"The dream of liberty." Andrew responded with genuine sincerity.

Emma Minton gave Andrew's hand a warm shake. "Come with me, please," she said. She walked to the back of the shop. She opened a door which led into another room. It was the part of the building where the seamstress lived. Andrew followed her into the room. She closed the door behind them.

"My name is Andrew Mott, Miss Minton," he said. "General Washington sent me." Andrew took out the secret letter and handed it to her.

The seamstress pointed to a chair in the corner. "Why don't you sit down? I know you've had a long trip."

Then as she opened the concealed secret letter, she said, "Would you like a cup of tea? The tea pot is on the fire and the water is hot."

"Yes, thank you, Miss Minton," Andrew answered.

"Call me Emma, and I'll call you Andrew. After all, we are both spies," she said with a warm laugh.

Andrew liked the seamstress right from the start. But he didn't much care to be called a spy. Even if it were true.

Emma Minton sat back in a large rocking chair to read the letter. "So, it's to be Princeton next," she said in a low voice. She read the rest of the letter without speaking again. Then she made tea for the two of them. She gave Andrew his tea, and they sat and talked for a while. It was hard for Andrew to concentrate because his eyes were fixed on the beautiful gold locket. Then Emma went over to her desk. She sat down and took out a piece of paper. She wrote her answer to General Washington.

When she finished, she came back over to Andrew. "General Washington must get this letter by tomorrow morning, Andrew. If anything happens and he doesn't get the letter.....I'm afraid many of our men will die if that should happen."

Andrew took the letter. "General Washington will have this letter by morning," he affirmed.

"Good luck, then," the seamstress said. "I hope we see each other again soon. God be with you, Andrew.

"Good-bye, Emma." He gave her a cheerful smile. He hoped he would see her again, too.

As he left the shop, Andrew again looked around to see if anyone was watching. The sky was starting to grow dark, and it looked like there might be more snow.

Andrew wanted to see his friend Nathan Chapman before he left. But now he doubted if he should. *Could he keep from telling his best friend that he had become a spy?* Andrew wasn't sure. And he had Emma Minton's secret letter with him. What if...? No, Andrew decided. He had better not push his luck. Many men might die if he didn't get the letter to General Washington. His own father might be one of them! After hesitating only moments, Andrew turned away from Nathan Chapman's house and walked toward the wagon.

The Trip Home

The snow looked like it was going to hold up for a while. Composing himself, Andrew felt better about spying after meeting Emma Minton. She had seemed so remarkably sure of herself and of *the cause*. So, Emma Minton was the Allenstown Spy. He would never have guessed it. The British had been trying to find out who the Allenstown Spy was for a year. Now Andrew knew the secret. And because he did, Emma Minton's very life was potentially in his hands.

As he walked toward his wagon, Andrew saw two people near it. He could make out one of them. It was Mr. Calhoun! The other person was looking up under his wagon. He couldn't see who it was. Then Mr. Calhoun saw him. He said something to the person under the wagon. When the other person stood up. Andrew could see that it was Cara Calhoun.

They must be looking at the axle, he said to himself. He knew they would immediately see that the axle had not been broken. Mr. Calhoun would know that he had lied.

Just before Andrew reached them, Mr. Calhoun said to Cara, "I want you to do two things real quick. First, go over to the Chapmans' house. Ask Nathan if his friend Andrew Mott has been by for a visit. Then you run over to Mr. Woolsey's place. Tell him everything I told you. He will know what to do."

"But, Pa!" Cara cried out.

"You just do as I say!" Mr. Calhoun said in a mean voice, and turning very red.

"Yes, Pa," she said.

Andrew saw Cara turn and leave. Mr. Calhoun must have told her to do something for him. Andrew knew that Cara was afraid of her father. But something was up. Cara would never run off without first saying hello to Andrew.

Mr. Calhoun gave him that strange smile of his, and said in an awful voice, "Why, hello again. Did you have a nice visit with Nathan?"

Andrew knew he had to keep himself under control. "As a matter of fact, no," he said. "Nathan wasn't home. I talked with his mother instead."

"Is that right? Not home?" Mr. Calhoun said. "Too bad."

Then he pointed at the wagon. "Cara and I were just taking a look at your wagon. Your Pa did a fine job on the axle. Why, it almost looks like it was never even broken," he said with a sneering laugh. "A real fine job!"

Mr. Calhoun waited for Andrew to answer. But

28

instead he just climbed up into the wagon.

"Don't go yet," Mr. Calhoun insisted. "Come inside for a minute. I want to show you something. Got a new plow. Just came in from Philadelphia last week."

Hesitating, Andrew looked up at the sky. "It's getting late, Mr. Calhoun," he said. "I really should be getting home. My mother and father will worry about me if I stay too long."

Mr. Calhoun stepped inside the front door of his store. "It will only take a minute," he assured. "I want you to tell your father about it." Now Mr. Calhoun was acting like an old friend, the way he did before the war had started. Andrew didn't know what to do. He had no time to linger about.

"Mark my words. This new plow will make your work real easy this spring. I know your Pa will want to hear about it," Mr. Calhoun assured him.

Andrew got down from the wagon. He would only stay a few minutes. Maybe Mr. Calhoun would forget about the faulty axle.

Andrew went back into the store with Mr. Calhoun. He told Andrew all about the new plow. It took a half hour to explain everything. Then when Andrew tried to leave the store, he stopped him at the door.

"Oh, I almost forgot. I have some pretty cloth for your mother. She ordered it some time ago, and it just came in. It will make a beautiful dress. I'll cut it for her. Just be a minute, Andrew," Mr.

Calhoun explained.

As he turned away from the door, someone on a horse rode past the store. It looked like Mr. Woolsey's horse. But the person riding it looked like Cara Calhoun. *Why would Cara be riding Mr. Woolsey's horse? Maybe it wasn't Cara. It was getting dark and he couldn't really trust what he saw...*

Another half hour passed before Andrew left for home. By this time, Cara had never returned to the store. But Mr. Calhoun had been very nice to him. Andrew didn't know what to think.

The trip home wouldn't take as long. The two horses knew they were going back to the farm, where they would eat and go to sleep. Together, they pulled the wagon down the road at a fast clip.

"Giddyap, Ginger, Giddyap, Dusty," he said. The letter from Emma Minton was in his secret pocket. Mr. Calhoun wasn't going to stop him from getting that letter to General Washington.

He smiled to himself. Not even the whole British army would stop him!

Captured

Cara Calhoun never dreamed a horse could be so fast. It was only the second time Mr. Woolsey had ever let her ride Lightning. The road that led to the Assumpink Creek flew by. Soon she would actually be in the camp of General Cornwallis.

Everything had happened so fast. Cara didn't even have time to think about what she was doing. First she had gone over to the Chapmans' house. Alarmed, Nathan said he hadn't seen Andrew in a long time. Then she ran over to Mr. Woolsey's place. Cara told Mr. Woolsey everything her father had told her to say.

"By the power of King George, we have got him!" Mr. Woolsey had shouted.

"Who have we got?" Cara asked cautiously.

"The Allenstown Spy, that's who! That little farm boy must know the name of the Allenstown Spy. He is going to give us his name, or else. General Cornwallis will see to that! Yes, sir, we have got him now," Mr. Woolsey said, half to himself, smacking one hand into the other.

As Cara rode toward Assumpink Creek she was

afraid for Andrew. She liked him very much. He was the only boy Cara could really talk to. And it was the look in Mr. Woolsey's piercing eyes that worried her most. She was afraid the British would hurt Andrew. She didn't want that.

Cara tried to make herself feel better. They won't hurt Andrew, she said to herself. General Cornwallis will just talk to him. They just want to know who the Allenstown Spy is.

Then Cara remembered how the British had hanged Peter Phillips. Cara had felt bad about it for a long time. She wouldn't talk to anyone and she wouldn't eat. She could only think about the times they spent together. But her Pa and Mr. Woolsey both said that Peter Phillips had it coming. He had been a spy and that was that. Cara really didn't understand what the war was all about.

Why did they have to hang him? Cara said to herself. They could have just put him in jail.

Suddenly Cara brought Lightning to a stop. The moon was starting to come up over the tops of the trees. *What if they hang Andrew like they did Peter? Cara pondered.* She gave Lightning's head a pat. "We could take our time, Lightning," she said to the horse. "That would give Andrew enough time to get back to the farm."

But then Cara thought about her Pa. She knew her Pa would be angry with her. Cara had gotten severe punishments before. Once her Pa locked her in the cellar for three days. Despite this experience,

Cara wanted to help Andrew with all her heart. But she was more afraid of her Pa than anything else in the world. Tears came to Cara's eyes. She shook her head slowly.

"I'm sorry, Andrew," she whispered. Cara wiped away her tears. "Giddyap, Lightning, Giddyap, boy!" Cara started out for Assumpink Creek. Once again the road flew by in the cold winter night, bathed only by a pale moonlight.

It wasn't long before Cara reached the British camp. She told a British soldier that she was from Allenstown. Cara said that she was carrying an important letter for General Cornwallis. The soldier took her to General Cornwallis right away.

The General's eyes grew hard as he read the letter which Mr. Woolsey had written. He finished the letter and looked up at Cara. "Do you know this young boy, Andrew Mott?" General Cornwallis asked Cara.

"Yes, Sir, General Cornwallis," Cara gulped and answered, almost in a whisper.

The General tapped on his desk with his hand. "Do you think he can tell us who the Allenstown Spy is?"

Cara didn't answer General Cornwallis. She felt afraid again for Andrew. Her eyes couldn't look at the General. Instead she looked down at the floor. She didn't know what to say.

General Cornwallis seemed to understand Cara's feelings. "No one will hurt your friend," he said softly. "But I must talk with him. It is men like the Allenstown spy who keep us from winning the war. Many British soldiers have been killed because of the work this spy has done. He must be stopped."

Still confused, Cara said nothing. General Cornwallis looked at her closely. "Cara," the General said, more warmly, "If your friend can tell us his name, that won't make him a spy. Do you understand?"

"I guess so," Cara said slowly, shifting from one foot to the other.

"Good," General Cornwallis said. "Then where is he now?"

"On the road to Trenton," Cara answered confidently. "But you won't hurt him will you?"

"No," General Cornwallis answered readily. "I just want to talk to him. Then he will be free to go home."

General Cornwallis called to one of his soldiers just outside the door. "Captain," the General beckoned.

"Yes, Sir," the soldier answered, stepping into the room.

"Take five men. There is a young boy riding along the Trenton Road in a wagon. His name is Andrew Mott. Bring him back to me as fast as you can," the General specified.

"Yes, Sir," the captain answered. "Right away, Sir!" The soldier left the General's office.

General Cornwallis turned back to Cara. "You've done a good job. Many lives will be saved because of what you told me. You are a fine young lady."

The General shook Cara's hand. "Why don't you sit here by the fire and rest a while?" General Cornwallis said. "If you like, stay the night. I'll have one of my soldiers fix up a bed for you in the cook's quarters."

"Yes, Sir. And thank you, Sir," Cara agreed, feeling weighted down by what was happening.

Cara was happier than she had been in a long time. Wait until she told her father what General Cornwallis had said to her. Cara went by the fire. She sat down in a chair. She began to feel like she did do something right. Before long, Cara forgot about her friend Andrew because she felt sleepy.

Andrew was cold and tired. And he knew his parents would be worried. But it would be two more hours before he was home. "Giddyap, Ginger, Dusty," he called to the horses, urging them on.

He came to the road that ran down from Assumpink Creek. Andrew knew the British army was up there. He made sure not to make a wrong turn. The last place he wanted to end up was in the British camp.

The moon was a bright, cold blue color. Andrew could see almost as well as if it were during the day. There wasn't going to be any snow tonight after all. That was for sure. He would take the letter from Emma Minton to General Washington first thing in the morning.

From back up the road Andrew thought he heard the sound of horses. It's just the wind again, he said to himself, trying not to shiver. But when he looked up, the wind wasn't blowing in the trees. He stopped the wagon and listened. The sound was still far off. It got louder as he listened. He knew it was the sound of horses on the run. There were several, maybe four or five.

Andrew's heart began to pound. "Giddyap, Ginger, Dusty!" he said. "Come on, giddyap, you two! Giddyap!"

The two horses jumped into a run. Andrew kept calling to the horses. Every so often he would look back up the road. All he saw was snow, trees, and a vivid winter moon. *Just a little more, he thought. If it's the British, they won't follow me too close to Trenton.*

"Come on, Dusty, run!" Andrew shouted. Finally he could see Walden's Pond. Once he reached the pond, he knew he would be safe. He took one more look back up the road. Suddenly his heart jumped. Six men on horses were right behind him.

"Oh, dear God!" Andrew cried. "Dear God! British soldiers!"

Andrew was going as fast as he could. But the soldiers were catching up.

Now Andrew had reached Walden's Pond. To

37

his horror, the British soldiers kept on coming after him!

Andrew's heart was pounding, and he knew that this was it. The first soldier caught up to his wagon and raised his gun. Then he called out to Andrew, "Stop or I'll shoot!"

Andrew pulled the wagon over to the side of the road. The rest of the British soldiers rode up.

"Step down from the wagon, please," the first soldier said. It was Captain Ewald.

When he got down, Captain Ewald pointed to the wagon. "Men, search the wagon," he said. Then to Andrew he said, "Are you Andrew Mott?"

Andrew answered a jittering "Y...y...yes."

"You will have to come with us," Captain Ewald ordered.

"Why?" Andrew said, staring ahead, trying not to wince. "What have I done? I'm just bringing supplies back to our farm."

"General Cornwallis wants to see you," Captain Ewald snarled. "We have orders to bring you back to camp."

Before he knew what was happening one of the British soldiers got up into his wagon. "You will ride that horse," Captain Ewald said. He pointed to the horse the soldier in Andrew's wagon had been on. "I must tell you, do not try to escape. We have our orders to bring you back to General Cornwallis. If you try to escape, we will have to shoot you!"

Andrew tried to look calm and in control, but

his heart was pounding and his hands were shaking. "Why should I try to escape?" he said. "I have done nothing."

Andrew got up on the British soldier's horse. The other men rode on both sides of him, their guns ready. Nothing more was said. They turned their horses back down the road toward the British camp.

As they rode along, Andrew started to think about Peter Phillips. Then he began to think about Emma Minton. He knew he would be brave for Emma. If they found out she was the Allenstown spy, they would hang her. He was troubled, but he started to feel less afraid. Thinking about Emma made him feel brave. Especially, thinking about all the men and women who were fighting for liberty made him feel brave.

Last Chance

The fires in the British camp burned strong and hot. Groups of soldiers sat close around each fire, trying to keep warm. The winter night was very cold. Andrew was taken to the small house that General Cornwallis used as his office. Andrew looked at the men sitting around the fires. Once inside the house, his eyes came upon a face he knew. Andrew had to look twice. He couldn't believe it. But there sitting in front of the fire was Cara Calhoun!

Had his own friend turned him over to the British? At first Andrew was so angry he felt like crying. Cara saw him and got up from the fire. She started to come toward him. Fighting back the tears, he felt himself become more and more angry.

"Don't worry, Andrew," Cara started to say. "Nothing is going to happen to you...."

But Andrew's face was red hot like the fire. He glared at Cara and his eyes betrayed his feelings. "I thought you were my friend," he said as his voice cracked. Then he turned to Captain Ewald. "Let's not keep General Cornwallis waiting."

41

Cara just stood there. "Don't worry, Andrew. He just wants to talk to you, that's all...."

Somehow, General Cornwallis was not like Andrew thought he would be. In fact, he seemed very much like General Washington. He spoke in a low voice with great control. He sat at his desk which was covered with maps and papers. On one end of the desk was an oil lamp, shedding a dim but steady light.

"Andrew Mott?" The General said in a commanding voice.

"Yes," Andrew answered slowly.

The General smiled at him. "Andrew Mott, I'd just like to ask you a few questions," he said. "Then you will be free to go home. You have nothing to be afraid of." The General looked down at the papers on his desk. "Now first of all, what were you doing in Allenstown?"

"I had to pick up supplies for our farm, Sir," Andrew answered.

"With all this snow?" General Cornwallis asked. "Did your family think it would be safe on a day like this?"

Andrew knew he had to answer the questions with great care. At this moment, he couldn't let himself be tricked into saying the wrong thing. "We were all out of supplies, Sir," he answered. "My Pa thought the snow was going to hold up. So did I. I always take the wagon to Allenstown for supplies."

"I see," General Cornwallis said. "Did you

42

know about the spy in Allenstown?" he asked him, letting the words come slowly, minute by minute.

"A spy? In Allenstown? Why, no Sir," Andrew lied. "I know of no spy."

He was putting on a good act. General Cornwallis came from around his desk. "Andrew Mott," he said in a firm voice. "I am talking about the spy in Allenstown who works for General Washington. He is called the *Allenstown Spy*. Do you know his name?"

Andrew could see that the General was getting angry. He began to worry. "No, Sir. I know of no spy in Allenstown," he said. *Then he thought, the General thinks the spy is a man. What should I do?*

The General's voice became harsher. "Is it that you do not know his name, Andrew Mott? Or is it that you will not tell!" General Cornwallis didn't wait for Andrew to answer him. "Captain Ewald!" he shouted.

The soldier came back into the room. "What did you find in Andrew Mott's wagon?" General Cornwallis asked the captain.

"Farm supplies, Sir," Captain Ewald answered. "There were only farm supplies in the wagon. Nothing more."

General Cornwallis tapped his foot on the floor. Andrew didn't know how long he could keep up his act. "Take off your coat," the General snapped.

Andrew followed the order.

"Captain Ewald," General Cornwallis continued, "take Andrew Mott's coat and search it."

Andrew felt sick inside as the soldier began to search his coat. He hoped against hope that he would not find the letter.

Captain Ewald searched the coat for several minutes but found nothing. He was about to put the coat down. "Just a minute," the captain said suddenly. "I think I've got something. Feels like a secret pocket inside."

Andrew's heart missed a beat. He knew if he found the pocket, he would find the letter next. Andrews heart began to lurch when Captain Ewald pulled out the letter from Emma Minton. He gave it to General Cornwallis. The General opened the letter and read it. There was a funny look on his face. Andrew could see that General Cornwallis didn't understand the letter. Emma Minton had used a secret code.

"What does this letter mean, Andrew Mott?" General Cornwallis asked abruptly.

"I don't know, Sir," Andrew answered.

General Cornwallis shook the letter at Andrew. "Who gave this to you?" General Cornwallis demanded.

Andrew looked around the room trying to think of something to say, and to be attentive and respectful.

"I ask you again, Andrew Mott. Who gave you this letter?"

Andrew was trapped, and he knew it. "I don't

remember, Sir," Andrew answered courageously.

For a minute, General Cornwallis looked mad enough to have Andrew shot! After a few minutes the General got himself under control. He sat down at his desk again. He did not speak for a while. Then he began to question Andrew again. He asked him questions for another hour. Andrew was tired and drowsy. He wanted to sleep even while surveying his surroundings.

Finally, the General got up from his desk. He walked over to Andrew and stood in front of him. "Do you understand what it means to be caught as a spy?" The General asked him.

"Yes," Andrew said slowly.

"I could forget that you ever had this letter....but you must tell me who the Allenstown Spy is," General Cornwallis urged forcefully.

Andrew was more frightened than he had ever been in his life. But if he told the General who had given him the letter, they would hang Emma. It was as simple as that. "Sir," he said. "I do not remember who gave me the letter. I do not know who the Allenstown Spy is."

General Cornwallis placed his hand on Andrew's arm. "Andrew," he said softly. "Is there anything more important to you than your own life?"

Andrew looked up into the General's eyes. He knew he was giving him a last chance. He was frightened but he answered in a firm voice."Yes, there is, Sir," he said convincingly. "Liberty."

For several minutes General Cornwallis could not talk. The great British general had never before known a young boy as brave as Andrew. "I see...." he finally said. "I'm sorry, Andrew Mott."

Then he began to walk from one side of the room to the other. "Captain Ewald!" he shouted. When the soldier came into the room, General Cornwallis looked at him with sad eyes. "Captain," he said. "You must be present while I sentence Andrew Mott."

"Yes, Sir," Captain Ewald answered nervously.

"Andrew Mott," the General said calmly, walking around his desk. "Your trip to Allenstown was most strange. You lied twice to Mr. Calhoun. You spent time in Allenstown with a person you will not name. A secret letter was found in your coat. You will not even tell me what the letter means. But most important of all, you will not tell me the person who gave you the letter."

The British general stopped in the center of the small room. He ran his hand in his hair. "Andrew Mott, I have given you more than enough chances to save yourself. I find you guilty of being a spy for the Continental Army under General George Washington. I order you to be hanged by the neck until dead. The sentence will be carried out tomorrow morning at first light."

The Reverend Taylor

Word was quick to spread around the British camp. A spy would be hanged in the morning. And the spy was a young boy!

Cara Calhoun couldn't believe her ears. General Cornwallis had said nothing dreadful would happen to Andrew. And now he was to be hanged!

Cara made her way around the fires that still burned. Many of the soldiers had gone to sleep. When she got to General Cornwallis' office, a soldier stopped her in her tracks.

"What's on your mind, young lady?" The soldier asked her.

"I must see General Cornwallis. It's very important," Cara pleaded.

The soldier just smiled at her. "I'm afraid that's not possible. The General has gone to sleep for the night. You will have to wait until morning to see him."

"I can't wait until morning," she said. "It's about the young boy who is going to be hanged. In the morning will be too late!" Cara cried out.

The soldier just shook his head. "First off, the

General has already decided to hang that spy," the soldier said. "Nothing is going to change that. And second, no one wakes up General Cornwallis once he goes to sleep. That's what I'm here for." The soldier gave his gun a pat. "Now you just go on off and get some sleep," he said gruffly. "Go on, now!"

Cara concluded she had to do something fast. After all, they were going to hang Andrew because of her. She ran to where Lightning was tied up. She told the soldier on watch that she had to get back home. Cara started out for Allenstown on the run. *If only there is enough time, she thought.*

"Come on, Lightning, move! Giddyap, boy, Giddyap!" she shouted to the horse. The miles flew by. Cara could think of only one thing. She knew there was only one man who could save Andrew now, the Allenstown Spy! But Cara didn't even know who the spy was. And morning was only a few hours away.

When she reached Allenstown, Cara went to the Chapmans' house. The house was dark. Everyone was sleeping. Cara had to knock for a long time before Mr. Chapman came to the door.

"Cara Calhoun!" He said. "Now, what do you want at this time of night?"

"It's Andrew Mott, Mr. Chapman. I've just come from the British camp. They're going to hang him in the morning," she said breathlessly. "They want to know the name of the Allenstown Spy. He won't tell them, so they're going to hang him."

Nathan, Andrew's best friend, came down the stairs. When he heard the news, he shouted, "The Reverend Taylor! He will know what to do, Pa. I've got to see the Reverend!"

Nathan pulled on his clothes and ran from the house. He didn't stop until he got to the Reverend Taylor's house. He pounded on the door until a light came on.

Reverend Taylor was still half asleep and groggy as he opened the door. "What is it, child?" The Reverend asked him in obvious surprise.

Nathan told him what had happened. "Can we save Andrew, Reverend Taylor?" He asked in a frightened voice. At first the Reverend didn't answer. He sat deep in thought. *The Reverend knew only one person in Allenstown who felt the way he did. He had talked in secret many times about the cause of liberty with Emma Minton. That's what must be, Reverend Taylor thought. Emma Minton must be the Allenstown Spy!*

"You must go home now, Nathan," he said. "I will do what I can."

Nathan looked at the Reverend with hope. But he shook his head, not looking at him. "Go home and pray for your friend Andrew. Go home. It is God's will which shall be done."

Reverend Taylor put on his coat as they left the house. He made sure no one was watching him. Then he walked over to Emma Minton's shop and knocked on the door.

In a few minutes he was inside, telling Emma Minton the news. When the seamstress heard that Andrew was going to be hanged her eyes filled and her face was soon covered with tears.

"There is only one reason you came to tell me this, Reverend," Emma said. "You must have guessed that I am the Allenstown Spy."

Reverend Taylor was slow to answer.

"It does not matter now, Reverend," Emma said. "I must try to save Andrew. Please wait one minute while I get dressed."

Emma Minton stepped into the back room. She dressed as fast as she could. Then she took secret maps and papers from a desk. Walking over to the fire, she threw them in. She must not leave any-thing important behind for the British to find.

That done, she went back out into the front room. "Reverend," she said, "I must ride for the British camp right away. The sun will be up in two hours. There isn't much time."

"I understand, Emma," the Reverend said. "You are a brave woman. You have given much more than most people for the cause of liberty. May God be with you, my lady!"

The moon filled the seamstress' shop with a soft, blue light. The two of them hugged, and then Emma Minton left. She had to make it to the British camp by morning. Andrew would be hung if she did not.

Emma had had a feeling about Andrew the first

52

day they met. Andrew Mott was the kind of young boy she yearned for as a son. But she knew that it would never be possible to have children now. The British would hang her first.

"Giddyap!" She shouted to her horse. Emma had no time to lose. *Her only thought was to save Andrew.* She must reach the camp by morning. It was cold but the sky was clear. Emma didn't feel the cold air. *She only knew how she felt about Andrew. She couldn't bear the thought of losing a child to the war. And it did not matter what might happen to her.*

Life and Liberty

It was just before morning when Emma Minton reached the British Camp. The soldiers were starting to get up. Some of them were already eating breakfast. The sky was gray and light snow was coming down.

"I must see General Cornwallis," Emma said to one of the soldiers.

The British general had been up long before first light. Emma was led to the General's office. For several minutes she stood facing General Cornwallis. General Cornwallis was intensely studying some papers on his desk. Finally the General looked up and spoke.

"Yes, what is it?" He asked the seamstress. General Cornwallis thought Emma was a member of Andrew's family.

Emma Minton looked the General in the eye. "You must not hang Andrew Mott," she said.

General Cornwallis looked at Emma in surprise. "Why must I not hang him?" The General asked. "He is a spy!"

The seamstress shook her head at the General.

"He didn't know what he was doing. Andrew Mott is not a spy. I have come to speak for him."

"Who are you?" the General asked.

"I am Emma Minton. To some I am known as the Allenstown Spy," she said all at once.

General Cornwallis got up to look at Emma. The General's eyes were wide with surprise. "I see," was all General Cornwallis could say. He had never known such a brave young boy and woman. First Andrew Mott had been willing to die for the cause of liberty. Now this woman stood before him saying that she was the Allenstown Spy.

"What kind of people are you Americans, Miss Minton?" General Cornwallis asked. "Does living or dying mean nothing to you?"

"What kind of people are we? We are a people who want to be free, Sir," Emma answered steadily. "We are a people who dream of *liberty*. And we will die for that dream, if we have to."

"A crazy dream," the General said. "But a grand one, too, I must say, to fill people's hearts with such feelings."

General Cornwallis looked Emma in the eye. "If only we could have met in another place and time, Miss Minton," he said. Then he walked back to his desk. "Miss Minton, I am sorry. But this is a war. I am a general of the British Army. You know what I must do."

Emma felt her heart sink. "I understand, Sir," she said in a low voice. "You have your side. I have my side. I am an American spy and you are a British general. Each of us has a job to do."

"I am glad you feel that way," General Cornwallis said. "You are a good and brave young woman. But war is war."

Emma Minton moved close to the General's desk. "Sir, about Andrew Mott," Emma said softly.

"You have my word, Miss Minton, as a soldier and as a man. Andrew will be set free. Captain Ewald!" the General called.

The captain came into the room. "Miss Minton," the General said. "Is there anything I can do before you are hanged?"

"Yes, Sir," Emma answered. "I would like to see Andrew one more time."

"You shall have your wish. But first I must sentence you," the General said.

Then General Cornwallis spoke in a low yet firm voice. "Miss Emma Minton, I find you guilty by your own words of being the Allenstown Spy. I order you to be hanged by the neck until dead in one hour."

General Cornwallis looked over at Captain Ewald. "Bring Andrew Mott here."

A few minutes later the soldier returned with Andrew. "Emma!" the boy cried.

Andrew and Emma walked towards each other slowly. They met in the center of the room. Andrew, in his boyish manner glancing to the side, hugged her tight. They both began to cry.

"Captain Ewald," General Cornwallis said. "Let's wait outside."

Andrew's eyes were filled with tears. "You shouldn't have come," he said. "I wasn't going to tell them who the Allenstown Spy was."

"I know, Andrew," Emma said. "but your friend Cara was so scared that you would die. You're too young. You have your whole future ahead of you."

After a long time Emma looked around the room. It was time to think about the war again. Her job was not yet finished. Neither was Andrew's. And they both knew it.

"Andrew," Emma whispered to him. "Did they take the letter from you?"

"Yes," he answered.

"Do you remember everything I wrote in that letter?

"Yes, I think so," Andrew answered, his heart sinking.

"Good," Emma said. You must go to General Washington right away. You must tell him everything I wrote in that letter."

Andrew looked up at Emma. "You have my word," he said. "It shall be done."

The door opened and Captain Ewald looked into the room.

"I'm sorry, Miss Minton. But it's time...."

Emma looked over at the soldier. "Yes, of course," Emma said, a bit shakily. Then she looked down again at Andrew, "There are two things which you must always hold dear, Andrew. *Life and Liberty*. Some say both are just crazy dreams. But you and I know better."

"Yes, we do," Andrew said. "And neither is so crazy a dream."

Andrew wiped his eyes with his hand. He reached up and kissed Emma on the cheek. Then he tried to smile while his heart plunged wildly.

"Good-bye, Andrew," Emma said in a soft voice. Emma took off the beautiful gold heart-shaped locket from around her neck. She placed it around Andrew's neck and softly kissed his cheek. "You best go now," she said. "You've been a great patriot."

Andrew held her hand. "Good-bye, Emma," he said.

Captain Ewald led Emma Minton from the room. She was taken outside and brought to the tree in the center of camp where people were hanged. The British soldiers took their hats off when Emma Minton walked past them. Even when men fight on different sides, a brave person is always honored.

General Cornwallis came back into his office where Andrew still stood. "Andrew Mott," he said. "You are free to go at anytime. If you wish, you may stay with Emma until the end. It is up to you."

Andrew tried to think of what Emma would want him to do. Deep down inside he knew. She would want him to leave right away for General

Washington. "I think I'll go home," Andrew said.

The General took off his hat to Andrew. "I understand, Andrew Mott," he said in a soft but steady voice. "I can only say that you and Miss Minton are both very brave. I hope that all your soldiers are not so brave. For if they are, England can never hope to win the war!"

They left the General's office. General Cornwallis walked with Andrew to his wagon.

"A safe trip home, Andrew Mott," the General said. "And may God be with you!"

As Andrew got up into his wagon, he could hear the roll of the drums. It meant that they were ready to hang Emma. He looked back to where the hanging tree was. Then he turned back to his horses. Andrew didn't know if he was brave enough to watch them hang the woman he admired. There were tears in his eyes.

"Giddyap, Ginger, Giddyap, Dusty," he called to his horses, his throat dry and hoarse.

As he turned down the road that led to Trenton, the sound of drums stopped. Emma Minton was no more.

Andrew drove for two hours before he reached the camp of General Washington. When he got there he told the General all that had happened. He wanted to cry again, but Emma wouldn't have wanted that. The General listened to his story without speaking. Then Andrew told him what Emma had written in the secret letter. General Washington looked at Andrew with great surprise.

"Andrew, words cannot speak to you my feelings right now," General Washington said. Then he put his hands on his shoulders and thanked him for his courage.

Turning to one of his men, General Washington said, "We leave for Princeton tonight!" Then he looked down at Andrew. "Would you like to come with us?"

He thought of Emma and quickly shook his head yes. "More than anything in the world, General Washington," Andrew said.

"Good," General Washington said. "Why don't you sleep for a while? You're going to need it."

"Yes, Sir," Andrew answered, his spirits now uplifted.

Late that night, General Washington gave the order. His men were to leave their fires burning all night while they marched on Princeton. The British would see the fires burning all night. They wouldn't think General Washington's Continental Army had ever left their camp. The British Army wouldn't be ready for the attack. Andrew was given a horse and he rode with the General. By morning they reached Princeton.

General Washington pointed with his hand toward the town of Princeton. Then he said to Andrew, "If we win, it will be because of Emma Minton." The General called out to his men in a loud, strong voice. "Men, begin the attack."

The whole Continental Army moved toward the town. The battle had begun and General Washington's men began to storm the British-held town. Guns roared on both sides. The air became dense and murky.

Andrew sat on a hill just outside Princeton. Indeed, he could see everything that happened. By late morning, General Washington's Continental Army had won the battle. The smoke from the guns cleared over the battle very slowly. And in the cold winter air, Andrew could feel Emma's spirit beside him. She had been watching the battle with him, and together they marked its progress.

Andrew listened hard, and he could hear her sweet, soft voice whispering like the wind. "There are two things which you must always hold dear," she was saying to him. *"Life and Liberty."*

Andy's Future

As the images all gradually blended, Andy was amazed to find out the history of the farm. He understood what his grandpa meant when he said, "The farm is worth more than a dollar amount."

The farm was rich in history and Andy's birth name was also rich in history. He was proud to be named after Andrew Mott, the young revolutionary and patriot, who at 12 years old played a major role in defeating the British. He also felt proud to be an American after hearing the story.

Andy and his grandpa sat on the porch swing enjoying the cool evening breeze as they watched his father and brothers come in from the fields.

Andy asked, "Do Rick and Dan know about this story?"

"Of course they do," his grandpa said without reservation. "It's extremely important to keep our heritage alive. And the best way to do that is by passing down our stories from each generation to the next generation. And the other way is to keep this farm alive with Motts."

"So Andrew started our heritage," Andy

recalled.

"Yes, and all the Motts after Andrew continue our heritage," his grandpa said meaningfully.

"That means I'll play a part in our heritage," Andy said, and a smile crept over his face.

"Andy, I am going to give you something very, very special. It's worth a lot of money, my boy, but it, too, has a value greater than money," his grandpa said.

His grandpa stood up and pulled a wooden box from his pants pockets. He placed the wooden box in Andy's hand. Andy slowly opened the box. Inside, lying on soft cotton, was a gold heart-shaped locket. Andy unlatched the tiny clasp. The words *Life and Liberty* were engraved on one side, and the words *Patriots Forever* were engraved on the other side.

"This locket has been passed down for 10 generations," his grandpa said. "I would like you to be a part of our family's legacy."

Andy felt warm inside and gave his grandpa a big hug. "I love you, Grandpa," Andy said.

"I love you, too," his grandpa responded.

Just then his father and brothers arrived on the porch. His father could see that something special had transpired between Andy and Grandpa Jack.

"You fellows enjoy your afternoon?" His father asked, sitting down to rest.

"Yes, Father. We sure did," Andy answered grinning from ear to ear. "I just learned about our

heritage and the importance of our farm."

Andy's oldest brother, Rick, who was going to college at the end of the summer, said, "We have all enjoyed many blessings on this farm. Now you know how important our farm and our heritage are."

Andy's brother, Dan spoke up, "Now that you are twelve years old, it's time you learned to work the land. Tomorrow you'll have your first lesson on the tractor. We'll need an extra set of hands during the harvest this year, since Rick will be off to college."

Andy was excited. "I can't wait to operate the new tractor."

"Not so fast, Andy," his father cautioned. You need to start off small. The John Deere 4620 tractor is just right."

Andy smiled. He felt honored that his brother wanted to work side by side with him.

Grandma Helen shouted from the kitchen, "Gentlemen, dinner's about ready. Please go wash up."

The Mott family sat down to dinner. The table was blessed with an abundance of food that was produced on the farm. There was a large baked ham, baked beans, cranberry sauce, yams, corn-on-the-cob, biscuits and strawberry shortcake for dessert.

Grandpa Jack said, "Let's all join hands and receive God's blessing and thank Him for this bountiful harvest."

"Andy would you honor our family by saying the prayer," his grandpa urged.

As Andy bowed his head, he was still thinking about Andrew Mott. Andrew was very brave and courageous. Andrew fought for *life and liberty*. Andrew was also kept safe by God's mighty power.

Andy, holding tightly to the heart-shaped locket, began the prayer....

What is Farming?

Farming is the most important occupation in the world. People essentially cannot live without food, and nearly all the food we eat comes from crops and livestock raised on farms. Of course, various industrial materials, such as cotton and wool, also come from plants and animals raised on farms.

Farming was once the chief way of life in nearly every country. For example, the typical American family of the 1700's and early 1800's lived on a small farm. The family raised cattle, chickens, and hogs. They grew corn, fruits, vegetables, hay, and wheat. Everyone in the family worked long and hard, but the results were often disappointing. Most families produced barely enough food for themselves. This situation began to change during the last half of the 1800's, and continued to change remarkably during the 1900's.

Scientific advance since the 1800's have made farming increasingly productive. For example, the development of better plant varieties and fertilizers has helped double and triple the **yields** of some major crops. Scientific livestock care and breeding have helped increase the amount of meat that animals produce. At the same time, the use of tractors and other modern farm machinery has sharply reduced the need for farm **labor**.

Farming is no longer the chief way of life in countries where farmers use scientific methods and labor-saving machinery. In these countries, farmers produce more food than ever before, and most other people live and work in urban areas. These changes have occurred in all **industrialized** nations and have been dramatic in the United States. In 1850, each farmer in the United States produced, on the average, enough food for 4 people, and most Americans lived on farms. Today, each farmer produces enough food for over 80 people, and less than 3 percent of all Americans live on farms. But even with the great decrease in the number of farmers, our nation's farms mostly produce more food than the American people use. The surplus has enabled the United States to become the world's chief food exporter. About a sixth of all food exports comes from American farmers.

As farming has become less important as a way of life in the United States, it has become more and more important as a business. The successful farmers of today are experts not only in **agriculture** but also **accounting, marketing** and **financing**. Farms that are not run in a businesslike way have great difficulty surviving.

The History of the Tractor

Tractors were first used during the 1870's. These tractors, called **tractor engines**, were large, four-wheeled machines driven by steam. They provided enough power to pull as many as 40 plows, but they were too awkward to be practical. Thus, smaller machines with **internal-combustion engines** soon replaced them. But the new machine, slightly different, had only a kerosene engine mounted on a four-wheel frame. Later, kerosene or gasoline engines were built as part of the tractor frame. The tractors could do almost all the field work but were too low to pull a **cultivator** through tall crops. Then, in the 1920's, the all-purpose tractor was finally developed.

Early manufacturing companies usually made only one tractor model or size. But more modern companies make a complete line. Modern tractors have both speed and power, and are easy to operate. Most have power steering and power brakes. Many also have enclosed cabs with heating and air-conditioning systems and special structures that protect the operator should the tractor accidently turn over.

The Parts of the Tractor

The tractor is a machine that pulls or pushes a tool or a machine over land. Tractors provide the chief source of power on most farms. They are also used for industry, military, logging, and highway construction. The tractor is powered by either a gasoline or diesel engine.

The modern tractor has several built-in features that enable it to provide power for other farm machines. These features include the drawbar, a hydraulic system, and a power take-off.

The **drawbar** is a device for fastening equipment to the tractor for pulling. The drawbar actually enables a tractor to pull such equipment as plows, wagons, combines, and hay balers.

The **hydraulic** system controls the working position of **implements** hitched to or mounted onto the tractor. An engine-driven hydraulic pump and cylinder provide power to raise and lower these implements. Many rear-wheel-drive tractors have hydraulic systems with a mechanism that shifts weight from the front to the rear wheels of the tractor. The weight shift increases traction for pulling mounted implements.

The power take-off, or PTO, provides power for machines that are either mounted onto or pulled by the tractor. The **coupling** device between the PTO and the equipment usually consists of two **universal joints**, one on each end of a **telescoping shaft**.

72

The flexible action of the joints and the telescoping action of the shaft together allow sharp turning and movement over rough surfaces without harming the power system. Overall, the PTO drives the moving parts of mowing machines, hay balers, combines, potato diggers, and spray pumps.

74

5. Big-capacity power brakes (regular) permit short turns at row ends.

6. Selector lever provides Load, Depth, and Load-and-Depth Control for hitch.

7. Position-responsive rockshaft operates in direct relation to control lever.

8. Power Differential Lock can be engaged hydraulically on-the-go for better traction.

9. Double-action remote cylinders control drawn equipment accurately.

10. Universal 3-Point Hitch handles both Category 1 and 2 equipment.

11. Posture seat adjusts to weight and height for greater riding comfort.

12. Hand and foot throttles provide a wide range of governed engine speeds.

13. Smooth power steering (regular) saves effort and fatigue on every job.

14. Hydraulic system offers up to three "live" circuits for implement control.

15. Selective control valve permits operating one or two remote cylinders.

16. Gas and Deisel engines across the board; LP-Gas, too, for "3020" and "4020" Models.

17. Front-mounted fuel tank keeps hoodline low for a better view of the work.

18. Oil cooler dissipates heat from transmission and hydraulic system.

19. Variable-speed engine provides husky, flexible power for every requirement.

20. Heavy clutch and flywheel help carry tractor through tough spots.

21. Dual rack-and-pinion steering motor turns front wheels at your command.

22. Exclusive variable-displacement pump provides hydraulic power on demand.

23. Exclusive Roll-O-Matic front wheels cut front-end bounce in half.

24. Power Shift provides straight-through shifting without clutching.

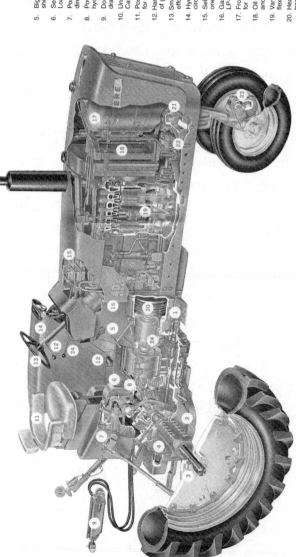

Take an Inside Look
at John Deere quality
and extra value

1. Front Power Takeoff delivers full engine power for 1000 rpm operation.

2. Sensing mechanism transmits implement signals to the hydraulic system.

3. Exclusive rack-and-pinion adjustment saves effort in spacing wheels.

4. Independent Power Takeoff handles 1000-540 rpm equipment.

The Types of Tractors

There are two major types of tractors: wheel tractors and tracklayer tractors, known as crawlers.

To illustrate, wheel tractors make up the majority of farm tractors in the United States. Many farmers use an all purpose tractor because it does a variety of jobs, such as planting, cultivating, and harvesting. It has high rear wheels. It has either one or two small front wheels placed close together or two front wheels spaced the same as the rear wheels. The spacing of the wheels enables the tractor to be driven between rows of crops. In fact, wheel tractors may have either two-wheel or four-wheel drive. Two-wheel drive models range in weight from about 3000 pounds to more than 20,000 pounds. Four-wheel drive tractors may weigh as much as 60,000 pounds. The demand for larger tractors has increased as the average size of farms has increased.

Tracklayer tractors or crawlers are driven on two endless tracks. They are steered by stopping or slowing one of the tracks. Crawler tractors are used for heavy jobs, for land clearing, and for work on soft or rugged land. In many instances, the smaller crawlers weigh about 3,800 pounds. The largest of these tractors weighs more than 70,000 pounds.

Vocabulary Words

accounting
> the system of recording and summarizing business and financial transactions in a book of accounts

agriculture
> the science and art of cultivating the sod, harvesting crops, and raising livestock

coupling
> the act of bringing together, a device that serves to couple or connect the ends of parts or objects

cultivator
> a device that consists of discs that is fundamentally used for breaking up the soil surface

drawbar
> a beam across the rear of a tractor to which implements are hitched

financing
> the act, process, or an instance of raising or providing money

hydraulic
> a device which operates when a quantity of water, oil, or other liquid is forced through a tube

implements
> a tool or machine forming part of equipment for work to be performed

industrialized
> society in which large-scale industry is dominant

internal-combustion engine
> a heat engine in which the combustion that generates the heat takes place inside the engine proper

kerosene
> a flammable liquid that is less volatile than gasoline

labor
> working employees of a business

marketing
> the art of selling in a market place, the bringing and sending of goods to market

tapered
> to become gradually smaller towards one end

telescoping shaft
> a shaft that extends out but is tapered so it does not bind

traction engines
> large four wheeled vehicles powered by steam

universal joints
> a shaft coupling capable of transmitting rotation from one shaft to another

yield
> the quantity of food that is produced in an acre of land